SONG of the OLD CITY

ANNA PELLICIOLI

illustrated by
MERVE ATILGAN

putnam

G.P. PUTNAM'S SONS

One morning, in a very old city filled with boats, people, prayers, and hot tea, a man hands you a flapping fish.

You say thank you and hold the fish tight, but it is gasping for water,

so you throw it back into the sea.
You're afraid the fisherman
will be angry.

Instead, he pats you on the head and waves to his friend the simit seller.

The simit seller hands you one
of her sesame rounds. You thank
her and take a bite, and the bread
is still crunchy and warm.

Soon, you're surrounded by seagulls. You break
off a piece and throw it into the air, and the gulls
take turns diving until your bread is all gone.

The simit seller understands. Her eyes twinkle as
she whistles across the street to the ferry captain,
who welcomes you with a smile.

From the boat, the city whispers something
you don't quite understand. The water shines
for you. The freight ships sing low. Dozens
of jellyfish dance in the depths.

After three bridges and one palace, you start to shiver, so a man with wobbly legs hands you a steaming-hot tea. You thank him, drop a sugar cube in, and stir the drink with a silver spoon.

A boy with an accordion plays a song that slows down the ships and quiets the dolphins. Around you, the other passengers close their eyes, humming the music.

When he's finished, the boy takes a
bow and holds out his hand. Some people
give him a coin, but you don't have any,
so you hand him the silver spoon. The
wobbly man winks at you.

The boy takes your hand and you run off the boat together,

past the captain, across the Galata Bridge,

to the entrance of the Spice Bazaar.

Everywhere you turn, someone hands
you something—a walnut, a bunch of olives,
dozens of candies that taste like roses and
stick to your teeth.

110 TL

When your pockets are full, the boy
leads you to a secret rooftop, and
you sit there eating and watching the
boats go from one sea to another.

You give him your last rose candy,

and he tells you the story of the
boy and the girl in the lonely
tower in the middle of
the sea. You think
maybe he knows
what the city was
whispering.

But before you can ask, the boy is up

and running fast toward the Grand Bazaar.

You run after him and look everywhere, behind carpets and lanterns and strands of gold, but the boy is gone, and you are thirsty and lost and a little bit tired.

Across the street, a man is
selling pomegranate juice.

With nothing left to give him, you share the story of your day, from the fish to the boat to the accordion boy.

The man splits the fruit and hands you the juice.

As you drink it, a tiny kitten rubs against your legs, trembling and meowing.

You take the straw out of your juice
and feed the kitten, until it's all finished.
The juice man strokes the kitten and
calls over to his wife, who kisses the
top of your head . . .

and leads you into
a hot room made
of marble.

She wraps you in a towel,
ties a knot around your waist,
and takes you to a tub,

where she scrubs you until the whole day is gone and there is only you and the water.

After that, she covers you in a blanket of bubbles, which makes you giggle and the wife giggle and her friend giggle and so on, until all the women around you are clean and giggling.

When you are dry, you put on your old
clothes and walk outside

just as the sun is going down
and hitting the rooftops.

The tiles look like the scales of a fish.

A song comes out of the sky.

It sounds like a gift.

So you say thank you, hold it, and let it go.

For my mother and father
—A.P.

For my dear family: my mom, Şerare; my dad, Şahin;
ablam Burcu; my aunt Şako; and my best friend, Zeynep
—M.A.

G. P. PUTNAM'S SONS
An imprint of Penguin Random House LLC, New York

Text copyright © 2020 by Anna Pellicioli
Illustrations copyright © 2020 by Merve Atilgan

G. P. Putnam's Sons is a registered trademark of Penguin Random House LLC.

Visit us online at penguinrandomhouse.com

Library of Congress Cataloging-in-Publication Data
Names: Pellicioli, Anna, author. | Atilgan, Merve, illustrator.
Title: Song of the old city / written by Anna Pellicioli; illustrated by Merve Atilgan.
Description: New York: G. P. Putnam's Sons, [2020] | Summary: "A little girl ventures through the old city of Istanbul, receives many kindnesses along the way, and practices the tradition of passing on what she receives"—Provided by publisher.
Identifiers: LCCN 2019045620 | ISBN 9781524741044 (hardcover) |
ISBN 9781524741051 | ISBN 9781524741075
Subjects: CYAC: Conduct of life—Fiction. | Istanbul (Turkey)—Fiction. | Turkey—Fiction.
Classification: LCC PZ7.1.P445 So 2020 | DDC [E]—dc23
LC record available at https://lccn.loc.gov/2019045620

Manufactured in China by RR Donnelley Asia Printing Solutions Ltd.
ISBN 9781524741044
1   3   5   7   9   10   8   6   4   2

Design by Eileen Savage | Text set in Charcuterie Flared
The art was done digitally in Photoshop, using a Wacom Cintiq.